Animal Stories

OM
KIDZ

An imprint of Om Books International

Reprinted 2013

An imprint of Om Books International

Corporate & Editorial Office
A-12, Sector 64, Noida 201 301
Uttar Pradesh, India
Phone: +91 120 477 4100
Email: editorial@ombooks.com
Website: www.ombooksinternational.com

Sales Office
4379/4B, Prakash House, Ansari Road
Darya Ganj, New Delhi 110 002, India
Phone: +91 11 2326 3363, 2326 5303
Fax: +91 11 2327 8091
Email: sales@ombooks.com
Website: www.ombooks.com

ISBN: 978-81-87107-81-1

Printed in India

10 9 8 7 6 5 4 3

Contents

Christopher's Day Out

It was Christopher's favourite time of the year. Cool breeze drifted through homes, colourful leaves adorned pathways and delicious pumpkins grew on the vines. Christopher ran happily through the cobbled pathway, enjoying the lovely weather.

He saw the corn stalks in the field. They were all dried up and crackly, and had taken on a light brown colour. It seemed they were on the verge of dying. He ran around the corncobs which were left and saw that they were turning quite hard too.

Mrs. Charles had just finished her daily chore of piling leaves. Christopher could not

resist the temptation and naughtily he hit the piled up leaves with his tail and up they flew, into the cool air, like the feathers of birds.

Christopher loved everything about winters —
even the smell of the leaves!

"Oh! There they are, finally!" thought
Christopher — those big, orange pumpkins,
lying on the ground. Soft skins with vines
around them. Yummy! They would taste great

as pie and with a dash of cinnamon, they would be the tastiest thing on earth!

There was one pumpkin, which had been carved by Mrs. Charles. It lay on the ground with the white seeds and pumpkin waste next to it. Christopher walked around the sticky pumpkin waste and made his way into the carved pumpkin.

The pumpkin was nice and spacious inside. It was tempting enough to spend the night in there. Relaxing inside the pumpkin, Christopher looked at Raymond, the cat, running around in the lawns.

Christopher smiled to himself thinking how silly Raymond was, as the cat ran to a pumpkin patch, and took a lick at the pumpkin waste. He pulled a face saying, "How awful it tastes!"

Laughing, Christopher thought of playing a trick on Raymond. He thought of scaring

the cat and started making sounds from inside the pumpkin like a ghost. "HOO HOO HOO," said Christopher softly, trying to sound as eerie as he could.

Raymond was startled. He looked around and his lovely soft fur pricked up in fear.

Christopher repeated the sound, "HOO HOO HOO ... " Raymond was now sure there was something eerie about the pumpkin patch. There was a ghost lurking in there!

Christopher was confident that he had scared Raymond. He said, "I am the pumpkin

ghost. I love to eat cats like you for dinner. Wait till I get my hands on you, hooo..." Raymond pleaded, "Please do not eat me, please don't!"

"I have an idea," said Raymond. "There is someone who will taste really good—Christopher the mouse. Catch him. He will taste really yummy." "But why should I eat a

mouse when I like cats?" said Christopher. Now Raymond was truly afraid for his life. He could imagine the pumpkin gobbling him up. "What should I do!" he shivered.

Raymond decided to run from there without turning around.

He ran as fast as he could, while Christopher enjoyed his little prank of

scaring him. He lay down in the pumpkin to relax and enjoy his soft, cozy seat. Mrs. Charles saw Raymond running into the house, surprised

to see him in such a hurry. The tubby cat normally lazed around all day long, soaking up the sun.

Raymond did not stop till he had reached the carpet. "You look really tired!" said Mrs. Charles, petting his white, silky fur coat.

Raymond was still trembling with fear, when Mrs. Charles announced she was going outside to bring in the carved pumpkin.

"When I get back, I will get you some nice, warm milk," she said. She went to the garden and picked up the pumpkin, which incidentally, still had Christopher sleeping soundly inside it.

"Raymond, here is your milk," called out Mrs. Charles. Raymond walked up gingerly to the kitchen, and saw the pumpkin on the table. He lapped up the milk as fast as he could and went back to his cosy carpet.

"Why is Raymond behaving so oddly?" thought Mrs. Charles. In the meantime, Christopher woke up and looked outside. He realised he was in Mrs. Charles' house. And to his delight, he saw Raymond lying warm and

comfortable near the fireplace. "Oh, what a great day for fun," he giggled. When Mrs. Charles stepped out of the kitchen, he shouted "HOO HOO HOO." Raymond got up immediately hearing the familiar scary sound.

"HOO HOO HOO," howled Christopher again. "Did you think I could let go of a plump, chubby cat like you?" said Christopher. Raymond looked up and screamed, "It's haunted! There is a ghost inside the house now!"

"There is the haunted pumpkin," shrieked
Raymond. Christopher decided to scare him
further by rocking the pumpkin and howling,
"HOO HOO HOO! Wait till I get you!"

Raymond could take it no longer. He was
trembling with fear. He ran out of the

door and did not come back inside for the entire day.

While Christopher enjoyed his time in the kitchen — nibbling on cheese and some

delicious corn as the fire crackled to warm him up. Christopher had found a nice place for winters and Raymond would surely be no trouble!

Emily's Lesson

The wind was blowing gently and Emily, the cow, was having fun in the field eating daisies. She ate other things like hay and grass, but daisies were her all-time favourite. She loved chewing on the soft, yummy petals.

She found the daisies on the banks of the stream, that she loved to visit. Every day, Emily would go to the stream to chew on her favourite daisies.

Later in the day, Farmer Noel would milk
her in the shed where she lived. It was said
that Emily's milk was the thickest, tastiest
and absolutely white in colour.

It was spring time. Emily awoke looking at the lovely sun and was happy for now she could go to the stream and eat her daisies. She has been dreaming all night about them!

As usual, she walked to the muddy banks of the stream looking for her daisies. She saw a big bunch of daisies and sat down to chew on them. But right behind them, were purple violets.

Emily had not seen the pretty violets yet as she was really enjoying her daisy breakfast. "Oh! How lucky I am to have daisies everyday," said Emily. After chewing on them for a little while, she bent down for some more, and lo! What did she see? Violets of course.

"What a lovely colour," she thought. "I must eat some. I am sure they'll taste just as good as they look." The violets indeed were really tasty. She spent the entire day searching for violets along the banks of the stream.

Purple violets were there everywhere — in the grass and in the reeds. Emily made sure she had eaten each and every violet in the

grass. That evening, she was waiting for Noel to milk her.

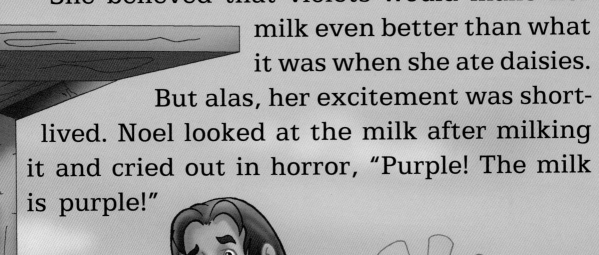

She believed that violets would make her milk even better than what it was when she ate daisies.

But alas, her excitement was short-lived. Noel looked at the milk after milking it and cried out in horror, "Purple! The milk is purple!"

"Emily! What happened to you? Why is the milk purple today?" cried Noel. Emily looked at the purple milk and realised it was because she had munched on those purple violets all day! "Make sure you do not go near those violets again," said Noel and put a stack of hay in front of her. But after violets, she had no appelite for tasteless hay!

When she woke up the next day, Emily could hear "Pitter, patter, pitter, patter," on the roof of her shed. When she looked outside,

she saw that it was raining. She decided to walk up to her daisies near the stream. On her way, she stopped by an oak tree.

Emily could see the stream flowing by from where she stood. But the downpour was so strong, that Emily could not move beyond the tree. She did not know what to do, as her hunger pangs increased every second.

The tree's leaves were too far above for her to reach out. The acorns were almost unreachable. Then she noticed something red a little ahead of her. She looked closely and saw it was a bunch of roses.

She thought, "It could not do any harm to eat one of those roses. They have such a sweet smell and look even prettier than the violets." Thinking that she made her way to the rose bush.

She used her tongue to get the first taste of the rose petals. She found them very soft and tasty. Quickly, she tugged at the bush and chewed up the roses. She thought to herself, "They are as good as the violets! Yummy! I should have come here first!"

Noel had forbidden her from eating violets, but he had not made any mention of roses. So she decided to go ahead and enjoy her treat. When she left the place, there was not a single rose in sight.

Emily looked up to the sky. There was no sight of rain anymore. So she walked home along the stream, with the sun shining on her coat of cream and brown. She was waiting to hear what Noel would say when he milked her that evening.

Noel came to her with the milk bucket. A few minutes later, he was shouting, "Red! This time, the milk is red Emily! What have you been doing?" Emily looked at the bucket and to her dismay, saw the red-coloured milk.

The milk had turned the colour of the roses she had so enjoyed eating the whole day. "Emily! You have to understand, I cannot sell red milk in the market. No one will buy it," said Noel.

He gave Emily a tap on her leg and led her back into the shed.

Next morning, she awoke with the firm thought that no matter what, she could not eat anything but the daisies near the stream.

But when she reached the stream, she found that Noel had cut down all the grass that had grown in an unruly manner. There were no daisies anymore.

Emily could only see nicely trimmed grass everywhere. She did not know what to do. After the rose-petal disaster, she had not eaten anything. She was hungry, and hay would just not do!

But there was nothing in sight that she could relish eating. Surely, the daisies would take many days to grow for her to eat them. She spotted yellow buttercups at a little distance, and decided to eat them instead.

Needless to say, the milk was yellow in colour. And so it was ... blue milk with bluebells, pink milk with pink heather and so on. Noel was getting furious by the day.

He told Emily that her milk was of no use
to him any longer, as it was in colours that
no one wanted to buy. How could someone eat
red cheese or pink curd? Noel made sure that
Emily understood how useless her milk was.

That night, Emily could not sleep. She was really unhappy and hung her head down, with her nose almost touching the dirt below. She cried and cried ... So much so, that soon there was a little puddle around her.

The next morning, Emily decided to try her luck one last time and walked to the stream. Suddenly, all her unhappiness turned into a bright smile. She jumped up with joy.

There they were — tall grass and little daisies! The nicely trimmed grass had not taken too long to grow back. She could not control her excitement. She chewed on the grass and the daisies like never before.

All along the banks of the stream, Emily chewed on every daisy she could see. That evening, she was eagerly awaiting Noel milking her. Noel had decided to ask her to leave, but he thought of giving her one last chance.

When he began to milk her, there came
the thickest, creamiest and absolutely white
milk that Emily was known for. "Emily! My
dear Emily! Now that's what I call milk," said
Noel, pleased with what he had on hand.

Emily was so happy at last. Looking at the white, creamy milk, she decided that she would never eat any flower, other than her favourite daisies!

The Song of the Birds

It was a bright, sunny day. A bluebird was sitting on a telephone wire, which was hanging from one wooden pole to the other. His feet were clutching the wires tightly. He was humming a melodious tune, as the clouds above drifted along quietly.

Hearing the tune, a red robin also flew down to the wire, right next to the bluebird. The bluebird was quite oblivious to what was happening. He continued humming his tune and the robin joined him in his song.

Not far from the wire was another tree, where there was a yellow canary. He had just caught himself something to eat, when the melodious song of the robin and the bluebird wafted through the air. The canary liked the tune so much, that he flew to the wire and joined the birds in the song.

As the song grew louder, with three birds singing it now, a brown thrasher, which was feeding itself from a bird feeder, heard it. The tune sounded very melodious and off flew the thrasher in search of where the song was coming from.

He could see the bluebird, robin and canary sitting on the wire and humming the tune. Soon, he joined them in their song. The other birds did not mind the thrasher joining them and they continued with their singing, as the white clouds continued to drift along.

A black crow was flying in the sky looking for something to eat, when the melodious tune got to him. He could see the birds sitting on the wire and singing the song. They were sounding very good! So the crow decided to find food later and instead joined the birds in their song.

A crow cawing sounded awful! But the other birds did not mind. When they sang their song, the crow whistled instead of cawing. And thus, the song went on with the five birds sitting on the telephone wire now.

Not far from there, a mouse was being chased in a field of cornstalks by a snowy owl. The owl's feathers were glowing in the light.

It was the mouse's luck that the owl heard the song of the birds. He found it so melodious that he stopped chasing the mouse and flew in search of where the song was coming from. He found the birds on a telephone wire and joined them.

The birds did not worry about who was joining them or leaving them. They simply continued with their tune, while the new entrant — the owl — whistled along.

A parrot was learning French when she heard the bluebird, robin, canary, thrasher,

crow and owl singing. "What a strange combination!" she thought to herself. But the song was indeed melodious.

She decided to let her lessons be and flew to the telephone wire. She sat next to the other birds, who were continuing with their

lovely tune. As they sang, the parrot whistled along and the white clouds drifted along ...

Inside a cage near the window, was a purple parakeet. He could hear the bluebird, robin, canary, thrasher, crow, owl and parrot singing. He too, found the song very melodious and

opened the cage. He flew over to the wire and sat right next to the owl.

The other birds did not stop. The parakeet whistled along, as the birds sang their song and the clouds drifted by. There was an orange oriole sitting on the branch of a tree, and trying to nibble on a ripe cherry.

The oriole heard the tune of the bluebird, robin, canary, thrasher, crow, owl, parrot and parakeet. She could see that they were all seated on a telephone wire, and flew to them.

The birds did not mind her joining. They continued with their song, as the oriole whistled along and white clouds drifted by.

In the meanwhile, a little girl and her mother were taking a walk and the girl happened to look up at the telephone wire.

"What an unusual sight mom!" said the girl, pointing to the telephone wire. "It looks like a rainbow of birds singing their happy song."

And there they were — the bluebird, red robin, yellow canary, brown thrasher, black crow, white snowy owl, bright green parrot, purple parakeet and orange oriole singing their tune as the white clouds drifted by.

TITLES IN THIS SERIES

   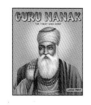